Say Thank You, Theodore

A Book About Manners

A Platt & Munk ALL ABOARD BOOK™

With love,
to Betty and Ed Lewison —W.L.

Text copyright © 1992 by Wendy Cheyette Lewison. Illustrations copyright © 1992 by Juli Kangas. All rights reserved. Published by Platt & Munk, Publishers, a division of Grosset & Dunlap, Inc., which is a member of The Putnam & Grosset Group, New York. ALL ABOARD BOOKS is a trademark of The Putnam Publishing Group. THE LITTLE ENGINE THAT COULD and engine design are trademarks of Platt & Munk, Publishers. Published simultaneously in Canada. Printed in the U.S.A.

Library of Congress Cataloging-in-Publication Data
Lewison, Wendy Cheyette.
   Say thank you, Theodore / by Wendy Cheyette Lewison ; illustrated by Juli Kangas.   p.   cm. — (All aboard books)
   Summary: Imogene tries to teach some manners to her uncontrollable little brother Theodore.
   [1. Etiquette—Fiction.   2. Brothers and sisters—Fiction.]   I. Kangas, Juli, ill.   II. Title.   III. Series.
PZ7.L5884Say   1992   [E]—dc20   91-33698   CIP   AC
ISBN 0-448-40476-1   A B C D E F G H I J

Say Thank You, Theodore

Theodore

A Book About Manners

by Wendy Cheyette Lewison
illustrated by Juli Kangas

Platt & Munk, Publishers

Theodore the Pest

Imogene's little brother Theodore was such a pest.
He interrupted people when they were trying to talk.

He ran around in restaurants. Sometimes, they had to leave—even before Imogene had dessert.

No one could relax when Theodore was around.

One day, Imogene said to Theodore, "Your birthday is coming soon. You're a big bunny now."

"Big bunnies know how to act," said Imogene.
"They have good manners."

Suddenly Theodore saw his friend outside. He ran out the door, letting it slam in Imogene's face.

"And I know just who should teach you good manners!" Imogene shouted after him. "ME!"

The lessons began at dinner, when Mama and Papa asked Theodore what he wanted for a birthday present.

"A frier enfin," Theodore told them.

"A what?" said Mama and Papa.

"Don't talk with your mouth full of food," Imogene told Theodore.

Theodore swallowed his noodles. "A fire engine!" he said.

Then he wiped his drippy chin
with his sleeve.
"Use your napkin, Theodore,"
said Imogene. "Like this.

"Sit up straight in your
chair— stop wiggling!

"You shouldn't grab. Say, 'Pass the
cheese, please,'" said Imogene.

Then she told Theodore to keep
his elbows off the table...

to keep his napkin in his lap...

and to stop slurping his milk
—it's not nice.

"And use your fork," she
reminded him.

So Theodore used his fork.
But he didn't use it the way Imogene had in mind. It wasn't going to be easy teaching manners to Theodore.

Playground Problems

The next day was bright and sunny. So Imogene took
Theodore to the playground.

Theodore ran straight to the slide.

"Me first!" he yelled.

"No, Theodore," said Imogene. "You have to wait your turn. It's not fair to everyone else if you go first."

Theodore went to the back of the line and waited his turn.

Then down he went—whoosh! Imogene smiled. There was hope for Theodore.

The next stop was the sandbox. Theodore loved digging in the sand. He loved his new red pail with the fish on it.

He loved it so much that when a friendly squirrel asked if he could share it, Theodore said, "NO!"

"If you share, Theodore, you can have more fun," said Imogene.

So Theodore filled his pail with sand. He let the squirrel use it to make a mud pie. They made lots of mud pies together.

Then they jumped on each one. Smash! Smash! Smash!

"See?" said Imogene. "Sharing IS fun!"

By now Theodore was very muddy and very thirsty, so they walked to the water fountain. A little mouse was trying to reach, but she was having trouble.

"She's taking too long," complained Theodore.
"Why don't you help her?" said Imogene. "Then she'll get done faster and you can have your drink. Besides, it's good manners to help."

So Theodore helped the little mouse. He pressed the
button while she stuck out her tongue.
"Thank you," she said.
Theodore just stood there.
"Say, 'You're welcome,' Theodore," said Imogene.

But Theodore was already getting his own drink. Imogene got soaked.

"Thanks a lot, Theodore," she said.

"You're welcome," said Theodore.

A Family Visit

The day before Theodore's birthday, Mama took Theodore and Imogene to visit the Quills. They brought homemade cookies with them.

In the living room, Mrs. Quill arranged Mama's cookies on a tray and passed them around.

Mama took one and said, "Thank you." Imogene took one and said, "Thank you." The Quill twins, Spike and Mike, each took one and said, "Thank you." Theodore took one and said, "Thank you."

Then he took another and another and another.
He said, "Thank you, thank you, thank you."
"Theodore," whispered Imogene.
"That's still not polite. You should leave
some cookies for everyone else."

Theodore took the cookies out of his
pockets and put them back on the tray.
But no one seemed to want any more.

Before long, it was time to go.
Mama said, "Thank you for the lovely time."
Imogene said, "Thank you for the delicious tea."
Spike and Mike said, "Thank you for the good cookies."
Mrs. Quill said, "Thank you for coming to visit."

But Theodore said nothing at all—because he was already out the door.

"You forgot to say, 'Thank you,' Theodore!" called Imogene.

"THANK YOU, THEODORE!" shouted Theodore. Then he was gone.

The big day was finally here.

"Now remember your manners, Theodore," Imogene told the birthday boy.

"I will," said Theodore.

But Imogene wasn't sure.

Soon Theodore's friends started arriving.
"Come in," he said politely to each guest.

They played pin-the-tail-on-the-donkey.
"You first," Theodore said to his friend.

Even when it was time to open the presents, Theodore remembered his manners.

"We can all play with them," said Theodore.

Imogene was so proud.

Soon Mama came in with the birthday cake.
Everyone sang "Happy Birthday to You."
Theodore made a wish as he blew out the candles.

Then Mama cut the cake.
"You get the first slice, Theodore.
You're the birthday boy!"
she said.

When the party was over,
Theodore said, "Good-bye and
thank you for coming," to each
of his friends.

Then Mama, Papa and Imogene gave Theodore their
birthday present. It was a shiny red fire engine.
"Thank you! Thank you!" shouted Theodore.
Theodore had good manners at last!

Well, most of the time.